CU00843087

The Elevator

A Short Horror Story

By Primary Hollow

Chapter 1

"Are you sure you don't need a ride?" Stella asked, flashing her snow-white teeth as her eyes glinted hopefully in the light cast by a lone lamppost.

"It's just a few blocks," Ethan said, smiling apologetically. "It's about time I get acquainted with the new city."

Stella sighed. "Well, just be careful. See you tomorrow then."

"Thank you. I will be. See you tomorrow."

The woman rolled up her car window and pressed on the gas. Ethan watched as her blue sedan crossed the empty street before taking a turn and disappearing behind tall apartment buildings. He lifted the collar of his gray coat and started ambling down the sidewalk, hunched against the autumn wind.

As the cold seeped into his body and he looked at the eerie shadows stretching from the narrow alleyways, Ethan somewhat regretted refusing Stella's offer. However, the undue attention from his new boss made him uncomfortable since he didn't want *things* to progress any further. At least not while he was still acclimating to the hustle and bustle of big city life.

"Maybe she's just being nice," Ethan mumbled under his breath as he crossed the street and stepped onto the road leading through the park.

"Yeah, right," his father's voice mocked him, rising from the depths of his consciousness. "I suppose she also gave you the position of her assistant just because she was *being nice*."

"Shut up," Ethan muttered while rubbing his aching temples.

"Yeah, who wouldn't want to hire a bum like you when you have such a fine record of taking nothing but odd jobs over the past two years," his mother jumped in.

An image arose in his mind of his parents standing in the doorway of their cozy family lodge.

His mother, Martha, had her arms crossed over her chest, looking at him disapprovingly. Meanwhile, his father, Joseph, furrowed his thick gray eyebrows, disappointment gleaming in his weathered face.

"You should come back home, boy," Joseph grumbled. "To the people who care about you. Come back home, or else—"

Ethan shook his head and took a deep breath, pushing away that commanding voice that had followed him ever since he decided to leave his controlling parents and make his own way in life. It got a little better after he started ignoring their calls. Still, their voices would occasionally come back at the moments of weakness, trying to convince him to abandon his dreams and return home with his tail tucked between his legs.

Ethan paused by a dilapidated park bench in the shadow of an old oak. He tilted his head, peering at the moonlight seeping through the labyrinth of gnarled branches, then took another big breath, trying to escape his brooding.

A cold gust of wind swiped past him, sending chills down his spine. Ethan shuddered as his gaze

3

drifted to the paved pathway crossing a crusty meadow illuminated by tall lampposts. The park seemed unusually empty, its stillness disturbed only by the creak of a rusty swing swaying in the wind.

Ethan pulled his collar up again, then continued down the road, feeling increasingly uneasy. As he approached the metal gates leading back into the streets, he noticed something moving just by the tall bushes framing an exit. Ethan stopped and squinted his eyes, realizing it was a large black dog, possibly a Doberman, similar to the one his childhood friend Rebecca would occasionally bring to their meetups. It was chewing on something greedily, producing sharp crunches and disgusting slurps.

Ethan glanced over his shoulder, then took a reluctant step forward just as the dog raised its head, revealing a bloodied snout with a string of meat stuck between its fangs. It seemed like it was chewing on some dead animal – possibly a raccoon. However, its attention was now fully set on Ethan as it opened its mouth and released a loud bark, spitting foam, blood, and half-chewed bits of skin.

"Easy there, boy," Ethan said, extending his hand while slowly walking around the dog. "I'm just passing by – no one is gonna take your dinner."

He was by the gates when, following another bark, the dog lunged, its bloodshot eyes radiating hatred for the person who dared to interrupt its meal. Ethan gasped and stepped back, withdrawing his hand just in time to avoid the dog's bite. "Stop it!" he shouted, hoping that his voice would scare the animal away. Unfortunately, it seemed to only make it angrier as, following another bark, it lunged again.

Ethan stepped back. "Stop!" he screamed before kicking the dog's snout. It yelped and dropped to the ground, fury in its eyes instantly replaced by fear. It then took off through the gates and across the street, barely avoiding a large white truck going way over the speed limit.

"Hey, what the hell are you doing!?" someone shouted.

Ethan turned to see three young men standing about thirty yards away. Two of them were clad in black hoodies, brown track pants, and dirty sneakers, while the one in the middle wore a worn black leather jacket and raggedy blue jeans.

"W-What?" Ethan mumbled, flustered.

The man with the jacket stepped forward. "We all saw what you did to that dog," he uttered in a raspy voice. "What are you – some kind of a psycho? Why would you kick a poor animal like that?"

Ethan glanced over his shoulder at the empty streets as agitation continued building within him. "I didn't mean to," he said. "It attacked me. I think there was something wrong with it."

"Yeah, right," the man scoffed. "I think there's something wrong with *you*." His hand slid into the pocket of his jacket, retrieving a shiny switchblade.

Ethan's eyes widened, and his heart started pounding in his chest. He froze for a second, looking at the three men walking toward him. He then turned and fled as fast as he could, feeling the adrenaline coursing through his veins.

"Hey! Come back here!" the man in the jacket yelled.

Ethan sprinted through the dim streets and

narrow alleys. He could hear the footsteps of his three pursuers behind him. Several people were walking by, but none expressed any desire to get involved as they stepped out of the way, refusing to acknowledge the desperation gleaming in his eyes. His breaths came in ragged gasps, and his chest felt increasingly heavy. With his strength dwindling, dark thoughts crept into his racing mind. He imagined the switchblade digging into his flesh, severing arteries, and splattering blood on the cold pavement.

Would they really kill me just because of the dog? Because I ran? That's insane! Then again – if they were people of sound mind, wouldn't they have already given up on the chase? Damn it, I need to lose them!

Just when he thought he couldn't go any further, his apartment building emerged ahead, its dark windows observing his frantic flee, just as indifferent to his plight as the people he passed. Ignoring the painful flutters of his heart, Ethan increased the pace, his legs barely touching the ground as he raced across the street, up the staircase, and to the large entrance door secured with a numeric lock.

He punched in the code with trembling fingers. After hearing a sharp beep, he grabbed the handle, leaped inside the lobby, and slammed the door shut, catching sight of his three pursuers climbing the stairs. Seconds later, they started hitting the door angrily on the other side, throwing curses and obscenities his way.

Ethan leaned on his trembling knees, wheezing, trying to catch his breath. The slams and shouts continued for about half a minute. Then, they abruptly ceased, giving way to an eerie silence disturbed only by the dull humming of the ceiling lamps.

He straightened his back, ambled to the dilapidated staircase, and a minute later was standing by the wooden door of his apartment on the second floor. Ethan rummaged through his pockets until he found a key, then unlocked the door and stepped into his shabby one-bedroom apartment. His hand instinctively reached for the light switch. However, he stopped at the last moment as a bad feeling washed over him.

Ethan closed the door and crossed the corridor into a tiny room. He tripped on one of many carton boxes scattered on the floor and almost tumbled but managed to grab onto the corner of the wall at the last moment.

"Calm down," Ethan muttered, then took a deep breath, carefully crossed the dark room, and peeked through the curtains. His heart fluttered uncomfortably after he noticed the three men standing in the shadows on the other side of the street, seemingly watching the building.

"What the hell is wrong with them?" he mumbled, then slowly withdrew and ambled into the bathroom. He turned the switch and peered into the mirror on the wall at his sunken visage and disheveled brown hair.

"That's just how the people in the big city are," his mother whispered into his ear, and for a moment, Ethan thought he saw her standing behind him. He shuddered, then rubbed his aching eyeballs, still trying to steady his racing thoughts.

I did the right thing by not turning on the lights.

They are bound to move on eventually, right? I should probably look for a new apartment and maybe change my clothes, just in case, but as long as I don't wander the dark streets, I should be okay... right?

Ethan sighed deeply, shaking his head. He turned the tap and watched the rusty bath fill with hot water. Then, he removed his sweaty clothes, climbed in, sat down, and closed his eyes, trying to push away the dark thoughts.

He was going in and out of the thick murk filled with strange shadowy figures carrying switchblades and baseball bats. He felt the bath water getting colder but was too exhausted to move, convincing himself to stay in for five more minutes as his head drooped onto the side of the tub.

Ethan was about to doze off when he felt something bump into his knee. He opened his eyes to see that the tub was full of blood, with bones and gory body parts floating on the surface. Gasping, he jumped out, slipping on the wet floor and splattering droplets of blood everywhere. At the same time, someone knocked loudly on his door, exacerbating his agitated state.

Ethan looked toward the sound, then shifted his eyes back to the tub. The gore was gone, replaced by murky water. He blinked several times, breathing heavily while holding onto the sink. "Just a dream?" he mumbled, feeling relieved but still baffled by the vividness of his nightmare.

Someone knocked on the door again, startling him. Ethan glanced one more time at the tub, then grabbed the towel and wrapped it around his waist before hurrying out of the bathroom and across the corridor. He paused just before the door, wondering who may be knocking at such a late hour. Then, he slowly leaned in and looked through the peephole, but there was no one on the other side.

Ethan stood still for a few seconds, then withdrew and was about to amble into the bedroom when the knocking returned, making him jump. He looked back wide-eyed, then approached and peeked again, but once more – the corridor was empty.

This time, Ethan waited for about a minute.

Then, with his heart thumping heavily, he turned the lock and stuck his head out, looking at the dim light of the ceiling lamps illuminating the dirty corridor ahead, lined with three doors on each side. He frowned and was about to go back when he noticed a yellow envelope lying on his doorstep.

Ethan bent over and grabbed it, then looked down the gloomy corridor again, shut the door, and ambled to his bedroom. He stepped to the window and peeked from behind the curtains. Although he didn't expect the thugs to be there, he was still relieved after only seeing several pedestrians walking by, wrapped in fluffy autumn coats.

He flicked the light switch and raised the envelope before his eyes. There was no stamp or address on the front – just his name, "Ethan," written in intricate squiggly letters. He looked at the writing for a little longer, wondering whether this was some kind of new advertisement. Finally, he opened the envelope and pulled out a blurry Polaroid of a young woman in a long green coat standing before a closed elevator. She was looking over her shoulder, presumably at the person taking the photo, with a surprised expression on her face.

Ethan leaned closer, squinting his eyes, observing her curly brown hair cascading around her slightly flushed face. Suddenly, he realized it was his childhood friend, Rebecca, to whom he hadn't spoken since he packed his bags and left his parents' home. At the same time, he remembered how he thought that the dog in the park looked familiar, which further added to his rising confusion.

Could Becca be here? Is she in some kind of trouble?

With his heart still thumping uneasily, Ethan approached one of many boxes scattered on the ground and rummaged through it before pulling out an old framed photo. It displayed himself on the left, his friend Gary on the right, and Rebecca in the middle – smiling from ear to ear. Ethan's heart trembled, seeing the youthful faces unbothered by the hardships of adulthood. He then frowned, noticing a yellow smudge on Rebecca's face. He tried to wipe it with his finger, but the mark seemed ingrained in the photograph.

Ethan's eyes drifted back to the Polaroid as he

examined Rebecca's surprised face – a stark contrast to her unbothered expression in the framed photo. The longer he looked, the uneasier he felt, wondering why someone would send him something like this. He put both photographs on the desk, then sighed deeply and mumbled: "What the hell is going on?"

Ethan rubbed his temples as his eyes drifted to a large red clock on the desk showing ten minutes before eleven. Hesitantly, he grabbed his phone from the nightstand by his unmade bed, opened his contacts, found Rebecca's name, and lingered a tad longer before taking a deep breath and pressing the button.

After several uneasy seconds, a monotone female voice spoke on the other end: "Your call cannot be completed. Please check the number and try again." Frowning, Ethan tried calling one more time but got the same message. He scrolled through his contacts until he found Gary's entry. He glanced at the clock again, then, nervously chewing his lower lip, pressed the button.

The phone beeped several times, and Ethan

thought about dropping the call when a drowsy male voice answered on the other end: "Hello? Ethan? Is it really you."

"Hello, Gary." He crossed the room and lay on the bed, trying to find the right words to tell his childhood friend.

"So... how have you been doing lately?" Gary asked after several seconds of uncomfortable silence. "I heard you're living in a big city."

"Yeah, something like that. How about you? How about Becca? I tried calling her, but she didn't pick up."

The phone went silent. A bad feeling washed over Ethan as if an invisible hand had wrapped around his insides and started to squeeze.

"Gary?"

"Rebecca is dead."

Ethan's heart fluttered painfully as he gazed blankly at the gray ceiling mottled with patches of black mold. "Dead? What do you mean?"

"She died in a highway accident two months ago," Gary said in a cold, emotionless voice. "I thought your parents had told you."

"My parents..." Ethan briefly covered his mouth, trying to control his breathing. "I haven't spoken to them in a while. Damn, you should've called!"

"How? Didn't you block our numbers? Besides, I assumed you didn't want to talk about it. It has been two years, after all."

"I-I'm sorry. It was never like that, Gary. I simply wanted to leave it all behind – to forget what my parents did to me. I didn't want to get you two involved."

An awkward silence descended once more.

"Gary?"

"It's very late, Ethan. I need to return to bed."

"If I come back, can we talk about this?"

Gary grew silent again before uttering: "Fine. Just let me know when you're in town."

The man's voice was replaced by a persistent beeping that lasted for several seconds before going silent. A plethora of emotions stirred within Ethan: sadness, regret, anger, and also – fear. His widened eyes drifted to the Polaroid lying on the desk. A chill ran down his spine as he tried to come up with a reason why someone would leave such a strange photo of his deceased friend on his doorstep. However, nothing he could come up with made even the slightest bit of sense.

Could it be my parents? Is this some kind of elaborate ploy to get me back home? Could they really be that crazy?

"Oh please," his mother spoke in his head. "Don't flatter yourself. Like we don't have better things to do than devise such petty schemes."

"Who else then?" Ethan mumbled. "Gary? He didn't seem particularly pleased to hear from me, so that can't be it. And what was Becca's dog doing so far away from home?"

"I thought you said that it *looked* like Rebecca's dog," his father grumbled.

"Still. Too many things just don't add up."

Ethan shuddered. Suddenly, it felt very cold in the room. He got up, dressed in his pajamas, then glanced one more time at the Polaroid before returning to bed and slipping under the sheets.

The sleep didn't come easy as he kept tossing and turning, thinking about everything that had transpired. It felt like it had already been days since he declined Stella's offer to give him a lift. He couldn't shake a bizarre thought that if he just went with her, none of this would have happened. That the thugs wouldn't have attacked him, the Polaroid would have never made it to his doorstep, and he would now be sleeping safe and sound, unburdened by the riddles of the dark.

Eventually, he drifted into an uneasy slumber filled with twitchy shadows, barking dogs, and photographs flapping around with Rebecca's concerned face peering at him eerily. He wandered that strange place until the shrill of the alarm clock vanquished his nightly terrors, announcing the start of a new day.

Chapter 2

"Ethan, are you listening?"

He flinched and turned to Stella, looking at him with penetrating green eyes framed by large red glasses. "I-I'm sorry," he said. "I had a rough night."

Stella tilted her head to the side and leaned closer, placing her hand on his shoulder. The sickening aroma of her perfume made him want to retch. Although he was never attracted to his boss, he could usually find some charm in her fading looks and confident demeanor. But today, everything about her repulsed him, from her bony hands and sunken visage to plump lips that she had a bad habit of smacking. All he wanted at this moment was to be far away from her and this decadent city infested with rabid dogs and murderous thugs.

19

"You know you can tell me anything," Stella said, peering at him intently.

Ethan hesitated, then uttered: "Yesterday, I found out that my friend had died in a traffic accident."

"Oh, I'm so sorry." Stella squeezed his shoulder. "Do you need some time off?"

"Yeah. I need to go back home. Just for a few days. If that's okay with you, of course."

Stella pressed her lips together, then sighed, getting up from her chair. "Sure thing, Ethan. I'll have to call someone to replace you, but it shouldn't be too big of a bother. Just let me know when you'll be back, okay?"

After Ethan nodded, she gave him one of her broad smiles, turned on her heel, and walked out of the room. After she left, he released a deep sigh, collected his things into his backpack, and ambled hurriedly out of the office. He stopped by an elevator, pressed the floor button, and watched as the red number at the top slowly climbed from one to thirteen.

After the doors slid open, he stepped inside,

selected the first floor, and leaned on the wall, tapping his foot anxiously. A part of him wanted to pack his bags and run from the echoes of his past. Somewhere far away – maybe into another continent. He was afraid that the sight of familiar streets and faces would stir up nostalgia, leading him to his childhood home, where he would once more succumb to his parents' will. He would forget his aspirations and stay in his hometown for the rest of his life, slowly whittling away while mourning the things that might have been.

On the other hand, he feared that by cutting his ties without making amends, he would lose a part of his humanity. That somewhere down the line, he would become just like his parents – uncaring and self-absorbed. And that thought was just too much to bear.

"You don't need to visit them," Ethan mumbled. "Just meet up with Gary, pay your respects to Becca, and then leave."

The elevator stopped at the sixth floor. Ethan stepped back to make room for whoever was waiting on the other side. However, the door remained closed. Frowning, he extended his hand and tried selecting the different floors with no response. He pressed the emergency button a few times, but again – nothing.

Suddenly, the entire structure trembled, and the lights above started blinking rapidly. Frightened, Ethan pressed the emergency button several more times. He expected any moment to hear a loud creak that would be followed by a free fall and then darkness, from which he would not awaken. The flickering madness gave rise to strange silhouettes, and for a moment, he thought that he saw *something* reaching for him with long, bony fingers.

"Stop it!" Ethan screamed. "I can't take it anymore! Just end it already!"

The elevator doors opened, and he was met with confused looks from the people in the lobby on the first floor. Ethan froze momentarily, his mouth hanging open and his heart pounding in his chest. He then hurried outside before the elevator could close and exited the building.

Taking quick steps, he headed toward his apartment building, keeping far away from the park and the shadowy alleys. It was still before noon, so the sidewalks were crowded with people, and cars were driving up and down the street. However, their presence did little to comfort Ethan's mind, which scrambled to blame his nightmarish sighting on stress and the lack of sleep.

It felt like he had walked for hours, flinching at every honk of a horn, constantly looking over his shoulder, fearful of seeing the thugs or the dog again. Finally, his shabby apartment building emerged in the distance, and minutes later, he was climbing the staircase to the second floor. Relief washed over him after seeing no strange envelopes on his doorstep. He unlocked the door, glanced down the empty corridor one more time, and went in.

Ethan frowned at a potent stench hanging in the air. Covering his nose, he crossed the hallway into the bedroom, where he stopped dead in his tracks. His widened gaze settled on a mutilated carcass of a raccoon sprawled on the floor, its dead black eyes staring vacantly at the ceiling.

Ignoring protesting grumbles of his stomach,

Ethan stepped closer, noticing bloody four-toed footprints going toward the ajar window. He hurried to close it, then turned back to the gruesome cadaver, trying to calm down and discern what exactly had happened.

Isn't this what that dog was chewing on yesterday? Did it somehow follow me home? And then what? Climbed to the second floor while dragging a dead raccoon between its teeth? That's absurd!

He looked warily through the window at the bustling streets.

Did those thugs somehow find out where I live and throw the dead animal inside to send some kind of a message? Seems a lot more reasonable, but... What about the footprints? Were they actually in my room!?

Ethan looked around frantically, his gaze pausing on the closed bathroom door. His hand slid to the knife in his pocket, but he stopped himself and grabbed his phone instead. With trembling fingers, he dialed an emergency number and waited until he heard an operator on the other end. Ethan quickly explained what had happened, gave his address, and started to wait.

He deliberated whether he should leave his apartment until the police arrived, but for the time being, he didn't want to go anywhere near the bathroom. He realized it was unlikely for the perpetrators to still be here, but considering everything that had happened recently, he didn't want to take any chances. Thus, he opened the window widely to give himself an avenue of escape and stood with bated breath, keeping one eye on the gloomy streets and one on the bathroom door.

Finally, Ethan saw the police car approaching and, several minutes later, heard a sharp knock. He hurried to open the door to find two uniformed officers on the other side. One of them was a burly man in his fifties. He had a long gray beard and a lush mustache. The other guy was much younger, tall and lanky, with thick eyebrows and piercing green eyes.

"Mister Ethan, I presume?" the old man grumbled. "I am Sergeant Ronan, and this is my partner, Officer Milton."

Ethan nodded and stepped back, letting the policemen inside. The old man pointed at the bathroom and gave Ethan an intent look. After he nodded, the officer motioned to his partner before unholstering his pistol and hollering: "Hello!? This is the police! If anyone is in there, come out with your hands raised."

They waited for several seconds. Then, Ronan motioned with his head, and Milton proceeded to kick the bathroom door open.

"What the hell?" Ethan heard after the tall man entered.

Ronan peeked his head in, widened his eyes, then turned back. "Sir, could you explain this?"

Ethan stepped closer and looked inside. A terrified gasp escaped his mouth. The floor, the walls, and even the ceiling were splattered with blood, and the bath was filled with murky gray liquid with fleshy chunks floating on the surface. Milton grabbed the mop from the corner and poked at them a few times before turning to his partner and uttering: "Rats. At least a few dozen of them."

"N-None of it was here when I left this morning," Ethan mumbled. A feeling of lightness washed over him. He wobbled, and Ronan had to grab his elbow to stop him from falling.

"Sir, are you okay?"

"Yeah. I just... need a minute."

Ethan returned to the bedroom, almost stepping on the raccoon sprawled on the floor. He slumped on his bed, holding his head with both hands, feeling like he was about to vomit or pass out – possibly both. With the oddities mounting, his desire to leave the city and return home was growing. Even the prospect of seeing his parents again didn't seem so bad anymore compared to the bizarre events unfolding around him.

Weren't they just trying to protect me from things like this? Didn't they tell me again and again about the evils of this world that target the naive and the unwary? Perhaps they just wanted what was best for me by mocking my desire to travel into the wide world.

Milton returned to the room with a phone in his hand and started taking pictures of the dead raccoon. Meanwhile, Ronan approached Ethan, giving him a thorough look. "Sir, do you know who might've done this?"

Ethan quickly recounted his confrontation with the three thugs while Ronan scribbled his description into a small notepad. After he finished, the old man released a deep sigh and asked: "Do you have anywhere to stay? If you'd give us permission to sweep the place, we could take care of this mess for you and gather the evidence in the process."

"Sure. I'll be out of the city for a few days – visiting my hometown," Ethan said with a surprising firmness in his voice.

Ronan nodded. "Yeah. That would be for the best. Although, from what you've said, I'm sure this is just a one-time occurrence. We'll still do our best to find these men, but without further evidence, we can't really pinch them for anything other than vandalism. Maybe animal cruelty."

"I would scratch that last part," Milton said.

"What do you mean?" Ronan asked, turning toward his colleague.

"This poor fellow has been dead for a few days

at least. I'm pretty sure it's a road kill – I can still make out tire marks on its neck. Wouldn't be surprised if all those rats in the tub are the same."

"Has anything like this ever happened before?" Ethan asked, raising his head, trying to keep his eyes away from the gruesome sight.

"I've been an officer for over thirty years," Ronan said. "I've seen things far worse than a few dead animals."

"I see," Ethan mumbled while tapping his foot, the desire to leave continuing to build within.

Ronan clapped a few times lightly on his shoulder. "I'm sure these boys were just trying to scare you – I wouldn't worry too much about it if I were you. Still, I think leaving the city for a few days is the right move. Let us take care of everything while you visit your hometown. Rebecca is waiting for you."

Ethan's eyes widened as he looked up at the Sergeant. "What do you mean?"

"These things have a way of sorting themselves out. If what you say is true – you don't really have any real quarrel with these guys. They'll just move

29

on to something else by the time you're back."

"No, I mean what you said about Rebecca."

Ronan blinked several times, seeming confused. "Who's Rebecca?"

A chill ran down Ethan's spine. He opened his mouth, then closed it again before finally uttering: "I thought you said... I..." He lowered his eyes and shook his head. "I'm sorry. I think I'm still in shock because of what happened."

Frowning, Ronan glanced back at Milton, then locked his intense gaze on Ethan again. "Do you have a spare key, sir? We'll call our forensics guy to take care of this while you are gone."

Ethan nodded, then got up on wobbly legs and approached his desk. As he reached for the drawer, his eyes paused on the Polaroid lying on top. He felt the lightness in his head again upon noticing that the elevator doors were slightly open, although he was pretty sure they were closed when he looked at the picture this morning.

"Sir?"

Ethan took a deep breath, grabbed the key from the drawer, and handed it to Ronan.

"Are you sure there's nothing else?" the Sergeant asked.

"Yeah," Ethan mumbled. "I'm just flustered. I grew up in a small town, and nothing like this had ever happened to me."

Ronan gave him another thorough look, then nodded, motioned to his partner, and they both headed toward the exit. "Take care, mister Ethan," he said before stepping out. "Feel free to contact us any time if you remember anything or if you see those guys again."

The door closed. Ethan stood still for a while, breathing the foul stench in the air. He glanced at the disemboweled raccoon one more time. Then, his eyes drifted back to the Polaroid. Taking deep breaths, he extended his hand and picked it up, examining the tiny gap between the doors with soft yellow light coming through, illuminating Rebecca's coat.

"I must be remembering it wrong," Ethan mumbled.

As he continued examining the Polaroid, he realized that it was a lot clearer, and the expression on Rebecca's face was no longer that of surprise but one of fear.

What if it wasn't the three thugs who broke into my apartment but the person who left the envelope? They broke in, trashed the place, and replaced the photo. But for what purpose? To drive me insane?

A persistent idea arose again that his parents were somehow involved. However, Ethan pushed it away, refusing to believe that even they could stoop so low as to orchestrate something like this.

But then, the question remains – who's behind it all? Should I call the police again and tell them the full story? Or should I just leave for a few days and hope it will all blow over?

Ethan pondered for a bit longer, looking at the strange picture and Rebecca's frightened gaze. Finally, he decided on the latter, afraid to be labeled a lunatic for bringing such details after the fact.

"The last thing I need is to get committed," Ethan muttered.

He shoved the Polaroid into his pocket, grabbed his phone, and called the station to book the ticket for the night train.

Chapter 3

It was already around noon when, following a hoarse bellow, Ethan alighted from the bowels of the metallic monstrosity that spat smoke from its stack. His head was throbbing. He didn't get a wink of sleep that night, haunted by the gruesome images of the day before. The train station of his hometown was almost empty, with only a few people sitting on the dilapidated benches, wrapped in their thick coats.

Ethan took the Polaroid out of his pocket and raised it before his eyes. His heart fluttered uncomfortably after seeing that the elevator doors had moved again since the last time he checked about an hour ago. Rebecca's right hand also seemed to have shifted into a different position – closer to her chest – as if she was recoiling from something she saw.

He kept telling himself that it was all just a trick of the eye. Some kind of strange illusion conjured by his anxious mind. At one point, he even considered throwing the photograph away. However, in the end, he decided against it. Partly because he wasn't willing to fully accept it was actually changing but also because of a crazy idea that the Polaroid would somehow find its way back to him again.

He left the station and started ambling through the gloomy streets. Ethan expected the feeling of longing to rise as he walked the familiar roads. He feared it would convince him to forgive his parents and stay in this little town despite knowing perfectly well that their controlling ways would end up crushing his spirit. Yet, what he got instead was a strong sense of disorientation.

Although he still recalled the general layout of the town, everything seemed different: the streets were darker, the buildings looked shabby and crooked, desecrated with markings and odd shapes graffitied on their walls, and even the people he passed seemed strange. Their faces were distorted by thick mist hanging in the air, and they eyed him eerily as if he were an outcast returning to the land he was banished from.

Ethan reached the edge of the town with tall metal gates leading into the graveyard. He felt increasingly anxious, bothered by the outlandish look of familiar places, and worried about meeting his old friend, Gary. Once again, he didn't seem happy to hear from Ethan when he called this morning. Still, he agreed to meet by Rebecca's grave.

Ethan pushed the gates open, producing a mournful creak. The mist was thicker inside the graveyard. Weathered tombstones and crosses stuck out of the white sea, casting gloomy shadows on the narrow pathways. A lone figure wrapped in a long black coat stood unmovingly beside a grave by the western fence.

Ethan paused, looking in their direction, still trying to calm his nerves, then stepped onto the gravel pathway and approached, tiny pebbles rustling under his feet. He stopped by Rebecca's grave, peering at the black marble tombstone with her name etched on the smooth surface along with the epitaph: "Shine brightly among the stars, beloved daughter, sister, and friend."

"Hello, Gary," Ethan spoke, trying to push back a big lump in his throat.

The man turned. For a second, Ethan thought he had made a mistake since the person before him barely resembled his former friend. He looked at least several decades older compared to the last time he saw him two years ago: his disheveled brown hair was intermingled with gray strands, his cheeks were sunken, and large bags hung beneath his bloodshot eyes.

"Hello, Ethan," Gary said in a croaky voice, smirking sardonically. "You're late."

"I'm sorry. My train got delayed. Gary, I... what happened to you?"

Gary chuckled. "A lot." For a moment, it looked like he was about to burst into tears, but he seemingly put a great effort into retaining that grim smirk on his face. He glanced at Rebecca's grave, then continued: "Nothing is the same since she passed. People told me to move on, but I'm not sure

I can."

Ethan raised his hand, intending to place it on the man's shoulder, but he took a step back, something peculiar flaring in his eyes. "I'm sorry for not being there for you," Ethan said. "What exactly... I mean..."

"I already told you over the phone – an accident," Gary uttered bluntly. "A horrible one. I was one of the people they called to identify the body. Damn. If you were there that day, you wouldn't be asking why I look the way I do. Almost nothing was left of her after she was run over by that damn truck. She was all... twisted and mangled. Hell, she couldn't even have an open casket."

Gary covered his mouth and turned away, his shoulders shaking in a silent sob. For a little while, they stood enveloped by a grim silence. "Maybe we should go somewhere else," Ethan said.

Gary turned around, rubbing his eyes with his sleeve. "I don't want to go anywhere with you," he uttered contemptuously. "The truth is that I never liked you, Ethan. I always thought of you as a pompous and selfish person. However, Becca never saw you that way. You were all she could talk about, and she would always smile when you were around. So, I kept quiet because I always wanted what was best for her. Because I always... loved her."

Gary took a deep, wheezing breath. As he continued, each word felt like a dagger sinking into Ethan's heart: "But then you left without saying a word, and the smile faded from her face. Despite your betrayal, she tried to find you. She was ready to go after you, but you didn't even bother to send us your new address. Didn't even bother to answer our calls. You... You made her do this!"

Gary lowered his eyes, his fists clenched and blood rushing to his sunken cheeks.

"I didn't know," Ethan spoke after a short pause, his voice trembling from sorrow as a macabre realization dawned upon him. "I was just trying to escape my parents. I didn't want to get you guys involved. I... Gary, I'm so sorry!"

"Doesn't matter now. She's gone. You should leave. I don't want to ever see you again."

The man was about to walk off, but Ethan grabbed his sleeve. "Wait!"

Gary turned, his eyes filled with anger. "Don't make me punch you. Not in front of Becca."

Ethan slid his trembling hand into his pocket, retrieved the Polaroid, and extended it to Gary. "Do you know what this is? Someone sent it to me two days ago."

The man's eyes widened, and his face rapidly turned from red to white. He yanked his sleeve out of Ethan's grasp, then stepped back, shaking his head while his mouth moved without producing any sound.

Ethan peered at him intently, feeling increasingly anxious. He raised his hand and looked at the Polaroid, realizing that the elevator doors were now halfway open, with a shadow visible of someone standing inside.

"Doesn't this look like one of those abandoned buildings we used to play in?" Ethan asked, then turned his attention back to Gary, who was inching away, continuing to shake his head.

"You should go," Gary uttered, the contempt in his voice replaced by dread. "Throw that damn thing away, leave on the next train, and never come back. Maybe it's not too late."

"Too late for what?"

Gary was opening his mouth to say something when he was interrupted by a loud bark. Ethan turned to see a black Doberman standing on the other side of the fence, staring at him while gnashing its teeth and spitting foam from its mouth. The dog barked a few more times angrily, then ran off.

Shaken, Ethan turned back to Gary, but the man was already behind the gates, walking hurriedly across the street. Ethan debated whether to go after him. However, he decided against it, spooked by fear he saw in his former friend's eyes. He shoved the Polaroid into his pocket, then glanced one more time at Rebecca's grave before hurrying out of the graveyard and heading toward the station, intending to board the next train.

Chapter 4

The rusty exterior of an old train vibrated as it spat black smoke from its stack that mixed with the fog hanging over the town. Ethan stood on the platform, his thoughts heavy with indecision. He tried desperately to come up with a way to make Gary understand how sorry he felt and assure him that he was not alone in his grief.

If I leave now, am I not just abandoning him again? Would such action not cause even more anguish, eventually leading him on the same pathway Becca was on? I still can't believe she could've done something like this. Just because I left. I... never knew she felt that way about me. Damn, how could I've been so blind!?

The train bellowed hoarsely, announcing its departure. With a trembling hand, Ethan grabbed the Polaroid from his pocket. Just as he suspected, the elevator door had moved again. The shadowy figure inside was now more noticeable, although Ethan still couldn't discern any of its features. The bigger change came from Rebecca's face. She seemingly no longer stared at the person taking the picture but instead peered right out of the photo, her tearful eyes begging him to stay.

"Becca, are you trying to communicate with me?" Ethan mumbled. "Are you trying to tell me something? Something you didn't get an opportunity to tell?"

The train bellowed one more time and started moving. Ethan watched it disappear behind the corner, then turned and headed back into the town, determined to set things right so that Rebecca's spirit could rest in peace. Although he had never believed in the afterlife, he couldn't find any other explanation for the bizarre events happening around him.

She must be calling out from the other side, not only to me but also to Gary. That would explain why he ran off after seeing the photo – he must've experienced some of the same things I did during the past few days.

The sun shone brightly in the gray sky, its rays clearing some of the mist and partly lifting the outlandish aura covering the town. Ethan felt a little easier, his sorrow replaced by the belief that he was brought here for a reason – that by not boarding the train, he had broken the cycle and stepped onto the path that would allow him to atone for his selfish act.

After walking for about fifteen minutes, he stopped by a white picket fence surrounding a cozy cottage where Rebecca lived before her tragic passing. It had a two-story red brick facade and a sloping roof with a smoking chimney. Ethan took a deep breath, opened the gates, and walked down a paved path crossing a crusty meadow. After stopping by the door, he raised his hand and pressed the doorbell, producing a sharp ding.

Ethan fidgeted nervously, looking at the bare branches of an old oak growing in the backyard. A memory arose of him, Gary, and Rebecca sitting under the tree, laughing at the joke he told. He tried to recall what it was about, but the vision faded away, leaving only a heaviness in his chest.

Ethan waited for about a minute and was about to ring the bell again when he heard footsteps approaching from inside. Shortly, Rebecca's mother, Julia, opened the door wrapped in a long flowery robe, a questioning expression hanging on her weathered face. After several uneasy seconds, her eyes widened, and she uttered: "Ethan? Is it really you?"

"I'm sorry for not coming sooner," he mumbled, lowering his eyes. "I just found out a few days ago."

The woman pressed her lips together, then stepped aside, motioning him to come in. After he did, she closed the door and ambled down the narrow corridor into the living room. "You want some tea?" she asked, glancing over her shoulder.

"No, thanks," Ethan said. "I just wanted to check on you. To see... how you're doing."

The woman shrugged, then slumped on the sofa, staring vacantly out the window.

"Is Robert home?" Ethan asked.

"He has gone out to get some groceries. He should be back not before long."

"I see."

Ethan looked nervously around the room, noticing dust build-ups on what used to be a spotless floor and several cobwebs dangling from the ceiling.

"Are you staying at your folks?" Julia asked after an uncomfortable pause.

Ethan shook his head. "I haven't seen them yet."

"Well, you should. They keep asking us whether you reached out. I know you have your differences, but they still care for you, Ethan. At least with Rebecca, I know I won't see her again. What you're doing—" A sob escaped Julia's mouth, and she covered it with her hand. "I'm sorry," she mumbled. "I shouldn't get involved."

"It's okay. I'm sorry they're bothering you at a time like this." Ethan's nervous gaze shifted to the staircase winding to the second floor. "Could I see Becca's room?"

Julia sighed, giving him a nod. "Sure. Help

yourself. I... need a moment."

Ethan looked at her intently, trying to find some words of comfort, but unable to. With a heavy heart, he crossed the room, ascended the staircase, and walked down a wide hallway to the door with the name "Rebecca" carved into the wooden surface. He paused, feeling his heart pounding, then grasped the handle and pushed the door open.

A strong odor of decay hit his nose, and for a split second, Ethan expected to see the cadaver of a dead raccoon sprawled on the floor. However, there was nothing of that sort – just a cozy little room with a carefully made bed, a couple of shelves filled with books, and a single desk with notes scattered on top.

Ethan stepped inside and closed the door behind him. Looking around for the source of the disgusting smell, he approached the desk and leaned over, examining several yellowed sheets of paper riddled with strange markings and diagrams. He frowned as his eyes drifted to the framed photograph standing on the edge, displaying Rebecca clad in a school uniform. A chill ran down his spine after noticing a sizable yellow smudge on her face. He remembered seeing a similar mark on their photo back in his apartment.

"Are you out there?" Ethan muttered. "Are you trying to say something to me, Becca?"

Something rustled, making him flinch. He turned to see a thick black book sticking out of the shelf. Slowly, he approached and took it into his hands, its leather exterior sending tingles through his fingertips as if it pulsated with foreboding energy. Ethan stared at the blank cover for a bit, then opened the book and started flipping through the yellowed pages.

His eyes widened, and he felt madness brush against his mind as he was presented with utmost depravities he never knew existed. He saw women being nailed to crosses and burned alive and men being torn apart by three-headed dogs. There were detailed depictions of torture chambers with corpses rotting inside iron maidens and bleeding torsos lying atop the wooden tables. Then, he came upon a section displaying strange misshapen beings, each more horrible than the last.

He saw fish-headed humanoids with scaly skin, grasping spears and tridents in their webbed hands, and a pointy black obelisk rising from the sea with a giant snake wrapped around its smooth surface. There were also strange cloaked beings with tentacles sticking from under their hoods. Meanwhile, many other beasts didn't even have a clear shape and looked like twisted amalgamations of limbs, mouths, and eyes floating in a boundless space.

The pages felt very fragile, and the book itself seemed like it was about to fall apart. However, the passage of time didn't touch the depictions of monstrous creatures that leered ominously at Ethan from their painted cells. He could almost hear the infernal whispers coming from their mouth, desiring to reach out and pull him into their domain.

His sanity dwindled with each turn of a page, but he could not stop. His logical mind, his inner voice, and even his parents screamed at him to close the book and run out of the room, but the allure of the unknown was just too hard to resist. Thus, he kept turning the pages, absorbing more and more of the forbidden knowledge in the form of ghastly pictures and intricate markings.

Although Ethan was sure he had never encountered such writings before, they seemed strangely familiar. As he continued reading, separate words and phrases started making sense. They spoke about the realms Beyond and the malice residing between the cosmos. There were also mentions of a deity known as the Purple Eye of Chaos and the Eternal Labyrinth, which was some kind of a hellish dimension trapping the souls of the damned.

The room grew darker, and strange shapes emerged by the window. Ethan's body trembled as he tried desperately to regain control, but his hands moved by themselves, turning page after page. He heard himself uttering words not meant to be spoken by the human tongue in a low, hoarse voice that seemed alien and demonic.

His memories faded, and for a moment, nothing existed apart from him and the book, soaring between the layers of time. He heard his spirit screaming in anguish as his essence was permeated with a boundless dread of being trapped in this state for aeons to come. But then, something shifted, and the infernal grip on his mind loosened.

The book slipped through his fingers and dropped on the floor, producing a low thud that reverberated through space, breaking the spell that took hold of his senses. Ethan remained still, looking blankly at the wall, taking heavy, wheezing breaths. He lowered his eyes to the accursed tome lying on the floor, closed. Right beside it lay a photo cutout of him taken about five years ago during his high school graduation.

Slowly, Ethan leaned over and grabbed it, looking at his own smiling face, then turned it over to see an address scribbled on the back in what looked like Rebecca's writing: "Willow Street, 6."

"Willow Street," Ethan said, then breathed a sigh of relief since he half expected that hoarse, creepy voice to escape his lips. "Isn't this that abandoned place where we used to play hide and seek?"

He turned the photograph, then spent a bit more time looking at his youthful visage and unassuming smile. "Becca, what the hell did you do?" he mumbled, then shoved the photograph into his pocket – next to the Polaroid.

Ethan glanced at the tome on the floor, deliberating whether to put it back on the shelf. The visions he experienced just moments ago now seemed like a distant memory of a dream he once had. He even felt slightly stupid that an old picture book had such an effect on him. Still, the dread lingered in his mind, and he decided to leave the tome alone in case touching it could once more conjure the bizarre state he was in.

Ethan gave Rebecca's bedroom one last look, then left through the door and descended the staircase. The living room was empty. He looked at the imprint on the dusty sofa where Julia had sat before he left. He then cleared his throat and called out: "Ms. Lewis, I'll be leaving now. Thank you for letting me see Becca's room."

Ethan waited a bit, then turned toward the exit to see the woman standing by the door. Her head hung low, her gray hair covering most of her face. In her hand, she grasped a large kitchen knife.

51

"Ms. Lewis?" Ethan mumbled, feeling chills running down his spine.

"It's all your fault," the woman uttered in a raspy voice.

"W-What do you mean?" Ethan asked, taking a step back, his eyes fixed on the sharp blade, glinting in the faint sunlight seeping through the window.

"Gary told me all about it. He told me why she did it." Julia raised her head, revealing her wrinkled visage distorted by a sardonic smirk.

"I didn't know," Ethan said, raising his hands. "I'm sorry. I would've never left if I knew how she felt!"

"Lies!" Julia screamed, her widened eyes gleaming with lunacy. "You took her away from me! You killed her, you damn swine!"

She lunged. The knife whistled through the air, just inches from Ethan's face. He took a step back, almost tripping over the sofa behind him. Julia released an angry shriek, then lunged again, but Ethan kicked her in the stomach, knocking her backward. The back of the woman's head smashed into the wall, producing a sickening squelch, and she dropped limply to the floor.

Ethan froze in shock, taking deep, heavy breaths. He observed a tiny stream of blood ooze from the woman's mouth, forming a puddle on the floor. His eyes drifted to the knife in her hand, and he was about to lean over and take it away when he heard the door opening. Moments later, a thick male voice exclaimed: "Julia, I'm home!"

A heavy sinking feeling enveloped Ethan as if he was having a nightmare he could not wake up from. He saw the shadow approaching from the doorway as his mind raced, desperately trying to come up with what to say to explain what had just happened. "What the hell are you doing?" reverberated in his head, followed by: "What are you – some kind of a psycho?" He imagined Robert grabbing the knife and coming after him. He could almost feel the blade sinking into his flesh and hear the man shouting: "It's all your fault! You killed my daughter, then you killed my wife. But now, I'll kill you! Yes, I'll make you pay for everything you've done, you damn swine!"

Ethan turned and ran out of the room. He

crossed the kitchen and a narrow corridor before bursting through the back door. Behind him, he heard Robert shouting something, but he didn't listen – just sprinted as fast as he could – across the meadow, over the fence, and down the murky street.

He ran for a couple of blocks. Finally, he stopped, panting, leaning on a lamppost with one hand. Ethan glanced over his shoulder, then looked around, realizing he was in his old neighborhood. His eyes paused on a modest two-story lodge about fifty yards away on the other side of the street – the place that used to be his home.

"Ethan?"

He jumped and quickly turned to see his mother stepping from behind the corner of an apartment building, holding a grocery bag. She seemed much older than he remembered. Her face was burrowed with deep wrinkles, and her back was hunched, distorting her previously-imposing stature.

"I didn't know you were in town," Martha said, taking a step closer. "You should've called."

"I just came to visit Becca's grave," Ethan

uttered, trying to steady his breath.

His mother gave him an intent look. "Are you going to come in? Father is home."

"I-I don't think I'm ready just yet."

Martha pressed her lips together. "I see," she said after a short pause, then took another step closer. "You seem shaken, Ethan. Is everything okay? Are you *sure* you don't want to visit us? Maybe stay for a couple of days. We kept your room just the way you left it. We have *a lot* to talk about."

A gust of wind swept past them, carrying an eerie wail of the police siren. Ethan shuddered and took a step back, peering at red and blue lights blinking in the distance.

"Talk to me, Ethan," Martha said firmly, looking at him with piercing green eyes. She suddenly seemed a lot taller, her firm voice echoing in foggy streets. "You know you can tell me anything. Did you run out of money? Did you get into trouble? Whatever the case – we're here for you. We always were. Even though you abandoned us and ran off, we never stopped loving you, Ethan. So... just come back with me, okay?"

An overwhelming feeling washed over him, urging him to submit to his mother's wishes. Tell her everything that had happened over the past few days and beg her forgiveness for what he did. However, something else stirred inside him, bringing all the bad memories into the open: all the times his parents belittled and undermined him, all the times they mocked his ambitions and aspirations, and all the times they beat him while he was growing up for even the slightest infractions.

"Ethan?"

"I'm not coming back with you," he uttered through clenched teeth, feeling anger flaring inside. "I'll never set foot in that house again!"

He turned and sprinted down the street. "Ethan!" his mother's desperate voice came from behind, but he didn't stop – just continued fleeing, guided by the shadows that took hold of his battered mind.

Chapter 5

Ethan ran until he could run no more. He collapsed on the cold pavement, gasping and wheezing, his body trembling from agitation. He lay still for a while, feeling the cold seeping into his body. Finally, he pushed off and got up, leaning on the side of a tall apartment building.

"Things keep spiraling out of control," he mumbled, peering at the desolate streets stretching ahead. "I should leave and never come back."

He pulled out the Polaroid again. It hadn't changed since the last time he looked, Rebecca's eyes still gazing out of the picture pleadingly. Ethan gritted his teeth, then looked around, observing tall abandoned buildings with boarded windows and walls covered in copious amounts of graffiti. His eyes were drawn to a rusty sign reading: "Willow

Street, 1."

"This is it," he muttered, then glanced at the Polaroid again. "Becca, are you out here? Did you really want me to come back to this place?"

He hesitated, feeling increasingly uneasy. Still, the rising dread wasn't strong enough to overcome the guilt festering in his heart and the desire to see his friend one last time. To tell her how sorry he was for not answering her calls.

Ethan started moving, his footsteps echoing in the thick white mist. It was getting darker with the faint sun rolling into its nightly slumber. The street he walked seemed vaguely familiar. In his mind arose a memory of him, Rebecca, and Gary running between the abandoned buildings, laughing, their cheeks flushed from excitement.

Looking at these structural abominations at the time invoked a childish wonder. This place seemed like their own little world where they could hide from adults and all the worries that plagued their daily lives. But now, seeing the shabby houses, Ethan felt nothing but sorrow for the long lost days.

He stopped by a twelve-story building marked

with a number six. It was different from the rest – even more decrepit and leaning to one side as if it was about to collapse. It was constructed from white bricks that had turned gray over time. There was no graffiti. Instead, shriveled black creepers ascended the wall, some of their branches slithering inside the open balconies. In the middle, gaping like the maw of a beast, was a large entrance with doors torn off their hinges.

It was very quiet. Ethan looked over his shoulder at the darkening streets. About fifty yards away, he noticed a strange shape standing by the building. It reminded vaguely of a dog, but he couldn't quite tell through the mist that seemed to be thickening by the minute.

A chill ran down his spine as he peered at the lingering figure. A horrifying idea entered his mind that it was there to ensure he wouldn't back out at the last moment. Then, an even more frightening and bizarre thought emerged that he was always fated to come back here – to the place of his childish wonder, defiled by the gruesome tragedy that befallen his hometown.

Someone tapped on his shoulder. Ethan gasped and quickly turned, but there was no one behind him. He looked at the shadowy figure again, then, on trembling legs, finally entered the building, unable to resist the call of the unknown.

He paused, peering at the darkness, dispersed only by the faint twilight seeping through the cracks between the rotten planks covering the windows. The air was stale, permeated with a potent odor of mold and decay. Squinting, Ethan made out a large rectangular area with a collapsed staircase in the back and a narrow corridor going to the right. There was also an array of rusty mailboxes on the wall to the left, some hanging open while a few were knocked down and lay on the dusty floor.

Trying to stay calm, telling himself that Rebecca wouldn't do anything to hurt him, Ethan crossed the hallway and stepped into the corridor on the right. His eyes widened, and a short gasp escaped his throat as he peered upon the same elevator that he had seen many times during the past few days in the accursed Polaroid lying in his pocket.

While the rest of the building was in a state of decay and degradation, the elevator seemed in pristine condition, its gray doors lit by a single lamp shining at the top. Ethan started approaching. His temples were throbbing, and he felt like he was about to pass out. When he was halfway through, a sharp ding pierced the eerie tranquility, making his heart skip at least a few beats. Moments later, the elevator doors opened.

Ethan half expected a shadowy figure he saw in the Polaroid to leap into the open and come after him. However, there was no one inside – just glinty gray walls, polished to perfection, illuminated by a soft white light.

"Becca, is that you?" Ethan called out, then waited a few seconds before approaching the elevator and stopping by the door. "Do you want me... to come in?"

Ethan waited a bit longer, then glanced over his shoulder. All his instincts were screaming at him to run, but he feared that whatever forces had led him to this place would continue pursuing him if he were to back out. "I've gone this far already," he mumbled. "What's the point of turning around now?" He took a deep breath and stepped inside.

A feeling that something horrible was about to happen washed over him as all the events of the past few days flashed in his mind, shattering his mesmerized state.

There's no way Becca would do this to me! I need to get the hell out of here!

He turned, intending to flee, but it was already too late. The elevator doors snapped shut, almost cutting off his fingers. Ethan banged on them several times, then looked around, desperately searching for a button or an emergency exit. However, there was nothing but uncannily smooth walls as if they were crafted from a single mold.

Taking short, panicky breaths, he pulled two pictures from his pocket. The blood froze in his veins after noticing a sizable smudge in the middle of his face – similar to the one he saw in Rebecca's photos. He shifted his frantic gaze to the Polaroid.

Something snapped in his mind, and his mouth opened for a silent scream after realizing that the picture was moving. Rebecca's frightened expression twisted and changed, her lips curving into an uncannily wide smirk permeated with malevolent glee. Meanwhile, her eyes turned from hazel to pitch-black and started oozing thick, inky substance. She gnashed her teeth, then lunged as if intending to leap out of the picture.

A muffled wheeze escaped Ethan's throat as he recoiled, slamming against the back wall, and threw the Polaroid to the farthest away corner. With stark terror gnawing at the remnants of his sanity, he watched the picture move and shake, exuding the same black ooze he saw coming from Rebecca's eyes. It formed a disgusting puddle that grew in size, moving toward Ethan's feet.

Suddenly, a sharp screech pierced his ears, making him wince. Seconds later, he felt the elevator moving. It went up, down, then up again before abruptly shifting to the right, almost causing him to tumble into the inky substance on the floor.

He leaned on the side, trying to keep his balance, but then immediately withdrew as the shape of a twisted face appeared on the wall, its mouth gaping open, trying to bite him. More faces emerged from the ceiling, along with ghoulish hands, all reaching toward Ethan.

He crouched on the floor, his body trembling from panic. Meanwhile, from the place where he threw the Polaroid, now fully submerged in black sludge, sprang a sinewy appendage wrapping around his ankle. Shrieking, Ethan kicked at it with his other foot while trying to push away, splattering the inky goo all over the place.

The elevator screeched again, then jerked backward, making Ethan drop to the floor. At the same time, the doors opened, and he rolled into a narrow corridor soaked in a dim white light. Gasping, he stumbled to his feet, then turned, expecting to see the horde of demons coming after him. However, the elevator was now empty – free from ghastly protrusions, appendages, and the inky substance, with only the Polaroid and the cutout of his face lying in the corner.

Still shaking, Ethan wondered whether he should pick the pictures up when, following a sharp ding, the elevator closed, and he heard a low hum, indicating that it was moving away. He stood still for a while, taking deep breaths, trying to make sense of what had just transpired. However, all his coherent thoughts were replaced by nightmarish visions and infernal whispers, speaking about the evil residing in the dark corners of the world and the eternal torture of those unfortunate to cross its path.

Finally, he turned and started ambling down the corridor. There were doors on both sides, marked with strange symbols on top. Ethan approached one of them, carefully grasped the cold metal handle, and tried to open it, but the door didn't budge. However, he picked up some sound coming from inside. With bated breath, Ethan leaned closer and put his ear to the cold surface.

It was quiet for a bit, then he heard again – someone shouting, seemingly in anger. Ethan hesitated, then uttered: "Hey? Is anyone in there?"

The door trembled. Ethan withdrew in fear. Meanwhile, an anguished shriek came from the other side, as if hundreds of people were screaming in shared agony. He turned and fled down the corridor as more doors started shaking and demonic bellows echoed all around.

His leg muscles were throbbing, and sweat poured down his face, mixing with tears of despair that rolled from his eyes. Seconds slowly rolled by, then minutes, and eventually, it felt like hours had passed as he fled down the narrow corridor with spirits of the damned shrieking from their places of eternal torment.

Ethan was about to pass out when the screams abruptly ceased, and the corridor led him into a wide hall. He collapsed on the black marble floor, wheezing and gagging, a string of drool dangling from his mouth. After catching his breath, he raised his eyes to about a twenty-foot-high wall with a massive mural of a strange creature painted on its white surface. The monster had an octopus-like head with tentacles hanging in place where its mouth was supposed to be and large black eyes that reminded Ethan of Rebecca's distorted face.

On both sides, steep railless staircases stretched up and down into the dark. Ethan rested for a few more minutes, eyeing the gargantuan painting, half-expecting it to come to life. Finally, he got up, ambled to the steps on the right, and looked below.

He felt an uncomfortable tingle in his chest after observing a narrow staircase zigzagging through the boundless space all the way his eyes could see. He ambled to the stairs on the left to witness a similar sight. After hesitating for another minute, he started ascending, deciding that there was no point in lingering in this desolate hell.

Ethan climbed slowly, trying not to look down, taking careful steps and making sure to stay in the middle of the stairs to avoid tumbling over the side. His heartbeat steadied, and the feeling of terror subsided, replaced by macabre thoughts. He realized that no matter what this place was, he was unlikely to leave it alive.

That is, if I'm not dead already. How can something like this exist in the real world? What is this place, if not some twisted posthumous realm?

After several minutes of climbing, Ethan reached another hallway. It was almost identical to the one he came from, but instead of the tentacled creature, the mural on the wall displayed a woman with messy black hair standing in a scarlet sea. Her

67

remarkably beauteous face was distorted by a creepy grin, exposing her sharp teeth, and her bony arms ended in beastly claws with very long, sharp nails. Ethan gazed at the painting, feeling the dread creep back into his mind, then resumed climbing.

Time passed as he battled the encroaching delirium, speaking in his mother's voice, telling him that it was all his fault. "Even after all that had happened, you still defy our will," Martha whispered into his ear. "Even today, all you had to do was admit you were wrong and come back home with me. However, you abandoned us again. Was it really worth it, Ethan? Was it really worth it, my boy? Everything you blame us for, we only did because we love and care for you."

"No," Ethan whimpered. "You got it all backwards! I had to leave because of what you've done to me. I had to cut all contacts because I knew you would never leave me alone otherwise!"

"How dare you talk back to me, you ingrate!" his mother screamed. "I am the only one who answered your call in this cursed place, and this is how you repay me? Fine! Be it your way! I'm done!"

THE ELEVATOR

Ethan wobbled, just barely stopping himself from tumbling into the abyss. He took a few deep breaths, feeling regret and sorrow wash over him again. "Mother?" he mumbled. But the voice that haunted him since he left his family home was silent, leaving him completely alone.

Sniffling, Ethan continued ascending for ten more minutes until he reached the third hallway. This one didn't have any paintings on the walls. Instead, there were three corridors going left, right, and straight ahead. After some deliberation, Ethan started ambling to the right while chewing his lower lip to keep his mind from racing.

The corridor branched and turned. He came upon more staircases along the way, going up, down, and sideways. Everything was drenched in deathly silence, and Ethan could barely hear his own footsteps, muffled by the heaviness of the air.

After what felt like hours of wandering, he turned the corner to come upon an elevator similar to the one that took him to this nightmarish place. A faint hope glistened at the back of his mind that this might be the way out. That the things he saw were merely a warning – a reminder of what awaits him in the afterlife if he keeps running from his problems and distancing himself from the people he cares about.

Feeling a tingle in his chest, Ethan started approaching. He was ten yards away when everything was engulfed by a horrific screech. All the lights began to flicker, casting ghostly shadows on the walls. Meanwhile, the elevator doors started to bubble and melt away. From inside, a ghoulish white hand emerged, grabbing the twisting metal. Seconds later, a grotesque monstrosity pushed itself through the gap. It looked like a living corpse with patches of pale skin dangling from its skull. It dropped on the floor, producing a sickening squelch. Then, it raised its head, leering at Ethan with hollow eyes, before opening its mouth full of crooked teeth and releasing a mournful moan.

The monster stumbled to its feet, extended its bony hands, and started shambling toward him. For a few seconds, Ethan watched the abomination approach, his mind stuck, unable to comprehend the horror ahead. Then, the foul, rotten stench reached his nose, finally breaking his shocked state. He shrieked and fled as fast as he could through the branching corridors and winding stairs. He heard the ghoul chasing after him, occasionally producing a sorrowful moan that dug deep into his mind.

Shortly, he reached the large hallway he came through and was about to descend the staircase when his ankle twisted, and he fell through the side. Screaming, he grabbed on the edge at the last second. His eyes shifted to the abyss stretching below as he dangled on one hand, his arm muscles throbbing painfully.

Whimpering, Ethan raised his other hand, grabbed onto the marble floor, and tried to pull himself up, but his strength was quickly fading. He felt his fingers slipping, and he was about to lose his grip and plummet into the inky abyss when someone grabbed his arm and pulled him upward.

For a moment, Ethan expected to see the monster leaning over him, about to sink its rotten teeth into his face. However, he was instead met by the frightened eyes of a woman with tangled brown hair. Ethan scrambled to his feet before uttering:

"Rebecca?"

The woman smiled and gave him a short nod, then stepped closer and embraced him tightly, pressing her head to his chest. They stood like this for a few seconds before she finally withdrew. "I knew you would come," she said, looking at him intently with deep hazel eyes.

"Becca... But how?" Ethan mumbled, then quickly turned, looking at the corridors ahead, expecting any moment for the ghoul to emerge and come after him again.

"Look at me, Ethan," Rebecca said firmly. "We don't have much time."

He turned back to her, feeling chills running down his spine from the coldness he sensed in her voice. "They told me you were dead. I... I was at your grave!"

Rebecca took a step back. "You left so abruptly," she said. "I didn't get a chance to tell you how I felt."

"I'm sorry. I didn't know."

Rebecca nodded. "That's why I had to find you. I knew if I could talk to you, I could convince you to come back. But you... are really good at covering your tracks."

"I'm sorry," Ethan repeated.

Rebecca chuckled grimly, then continued: "I even considered borrowing some money and hiring a private investigator. But then I found it. During one of my long morning walks in the ruins of the house that we used to play by. You remember the one with the slanted wall and a large patch of poison ivy beside it?"

"Yes, but Rebecca, what does it have to do—"

"We never went inside," she interrupted. "I think even then, we could sense the dark aura radiating from its decaying carcass as if some foul presence had watched over us all those years, awaiting the opportunity to snatch us away. And that opportunity came on that fated day, on a cold morning as I ambled through the abandoned streets, my heart heavy with indecision."

Rebecca chuckled again, then continued: "I heard something rustling inside and stepped through the collapsed doorway. I found it lying in the middle of the hallway – waiting for me to pick it up. You know what I'm talking about, right? You also felt its dark presence."

Ethan nodded, thinking about the ghastly tome he discovered in Rebecca's room as uneasiness replaced the temporal relief he got from seeing his friend again.

"It talked to me," the woman said with a strange elation and pride in her voice. "I couldn't understand it at first, but then, little by little, the secrets of the forbidden tongue were revealed to me. They told me what I must do to fulfill my deepest desire. However, they withheld the cost of such a sinister act."

Rebecca's body twitched uncannily, and the right corner of her lip drooped slightly. She took a deep, wheezing breath, then resumed talking, her voice hoarse, as if she had something stuck in her mouth: "I didn't realize what I was doing until it was too late. I unleashed something that can never be contained."

"We can still get out of here!" Ethan exclaimed. "Rebecca, please. Is this really what you wished for?"

"I just wanted to see you again," she mumbled, tears welling in her eyes.

Ethan glanced at the empty corridor again, then grabbed her by the hand. "Come on, there must be some way to escape this place."

"There isn't. It will make you choose, and then it will spread until it envelops the entire world. Until the sky turns red and the Sleeper awakens to bend humanity to its will."

A sardonic smirk on Rebecca's face suddenly turned into an expression of utmost despair. Her eyes popped out of their sockets, giving way to hollow black holes, and her teeth started decaying rapidly, turning into gruesome yellow fangs. Horrified, Ethan tried to step away, but her bony fingers dug into his hand, holding him in place.

Rebecca opened her mouth widely, producing a sickening rattle as if her jaw was breaking apart. From the gaping maw, a sinewy tentacle emerged. It wrapped around Ethan's neck and started to squeeze as he struggled desperately, feeling the madness of the cosmos encroaching upon his mind.

The hallway disappeared. He floated inside the

void while some malicious force dug through his memories, occasionally pushing the images of places and people he knew into the surface that rippled through that boundless space. Finally, it released its grasp, producing a disgusting slurping sound as if he was being expelled from the belly of an infernal beast.

A frigid cold embraced his skin. Shivering, Ethan opened his eyes to find himself standing naked in the middle of the highway. Before he could understand what was happening, he was startled by a sharp toot of a car horn. He turned to see a large white truck speeding in his direction with a twisted, shadowy figure sitting behind the wheel.

Before he could react, the front of the truck smashed into his body, tearing it apart and splattering his insides. An excruciating pain briefly flared through his mangled flesh. Then, his head smashed into the cold pavement, and he was thrown back into the boundless dark filled with moaning ghouls, writhing tendrils, and the mad gods of the cosmos that watched his spirit fade between the looms of time.

Chapter 6

"Will you go to the funeral?" Bernard asked.

Stella sighed, leaning back in her chair, then shook her head. "I normally would, but I'm swamped, and it's so far away. That poor boy. It broke my heart to hear what he did to himself. I just wish I got to know him better. I noticed some sadness about him but had no idea he was this unhappy."

Bernard nodded, then stepped closer and put a yellow envelope on her desk. "This came for you this morning."

Stella's eyes shifted to her name written in intricate squiggly letters. "From whom?"

Bernard shrugged. "There's no return address."

Stella looked at the envelope for a few more seconds, then sighed, getting up from her chair.

"Strange. Anyway, I'll check it after lunch. Would you like to come with me?"

"Sure."

Smiling, Stella grabbed her coat and followed her new assistant out of the room, leaving the envelope on her desk.

Thank you so much for reading!

I hope you enjoyed the book. If you did, please take a minute to rate and share your review on Amazon. Writing means everything to me, and reader feedback helps me improve and reach a wider audience, contributing to my dream of writing full-time.

Printed in Great Britain
by Amazon

45343010R00047